This book belongs to:

....

Note to parents and carers

Read it yourself is a series of classic, traditional tales, written in a simple way to give children a confident and successful start to reading.

Each book is carefully structured to include many high-frequency words that are vital for first reading. The sentences on each page are supported closely by pictures to help with reading, and to offer lively details to talk about.

The books are graded into four levels that progressively introduce wider vocabulary and longer stories as a reader's ability grows.

Ideas for use

- Begin by looking through the book and talking about the pictures. Has your child heard this story before?

- Help your child with any words he does not know, either by helping him to sound them out or supplying them yourself.

- Developing readers can be concentrating so hard on the words that they sometimes don't fully grasp the meaning of what they're reading. Answering the puzzle questions on pages 30 and 31 will help with understanding.

Beginner readers need plenty of encouragement.

Level 1 is ideal for children who have received some initial reading instruction. Each story is told very simply, using a small number of frequently repeated words.

Special features:

The mother

The old woman

The magic porridge pot

The little girl

Careful match between story and pictures

Opening pages introduce key story words

Soon the kitchen was full of porridge. And still the magic porridge pot went on cooking.

Large, clear type

6

7

18

19

Educational Consultant: Geraldine Taylor

A catalogue record for this book is available from the British Library

Published by Ladybird Books Ltd
80 Strand, London, WC2R 0RL
A Penguin Company

004 - 10 9 8 7 6 5 4
© LADYBIRD BOOKS LTD MMX
LADYBIRD and the device of a Ladybird are trademarks of Ladybird Books Ltd

ISBN: 978-1-40930-354-1

Printed in China

The Magic
Porridge Pot

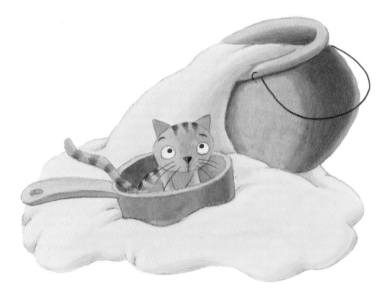

Illustrated by Laura Barella

The old woman

The little girl

The mother

The magic porridge pot

Once upon a time, a little girl met an old woman.

The old woman gave her a magic porridge pot.

9

"Cook, little pot, cook," said the old woman.

And the little pot cooked some porridge.

"Stop, little pot, stop," said the old woman.

And the little pot stopped cooking.

The little girl took the
magic porridge pot
to her mother.

"Cook, little pot, cook,"
said the little girl's mother.

And the little pot cooked
some porridge.

17

Soon the kitchen
was full of porridge.

And still the magic
porridge pot went
on cooking.

19

Soon the house was full of porridge.

And still the magic porridge pot went on cooking.

Soon the street was full of porridge.

And still the magic porridge pot went on cooking.

Soon the whole town was full of porridge.

And still the magic porridge pot went on cooking.

25

"Stop, little pot, stop," said the little girl.

At last the magic porridge pot stopped cooking.

But the whole town is still eating porridge!

How much do you remember about the story of The Magic Porridge Pot? Answer these questions and find out!

- Who gives the magic porridge pot to the little girl?

- What does the old woman say to make the pot start cooking?

- What does the little girl say to make the pot stop cooking?

Look at the pictures from the story and say the order they should go in.

A

B

C

D

Read it yourself
with Ladybird

The Three Billy Goats Gruff

Cinderella

Little Red Hen

Goldilocks and the Three Bears

The Magic Porridge Pot

The Ugly Duckling

The Gingerbread Man

Sleeping Beauty

Sly Fox and Red Hen

The Three Little Pigs

Town Mouse and Country Mouse

Little Red Riding Hood

The Elves and the Shoemaker

Jack and the Beanstalk

The Pied Piper of Hamelin

The Wizard of Oz

Collect all the titles in the series.